David Elliott

FOREVER AND EVER

David Elliott is the author of many picture books and novels for young people, including the *New York Times* bestselling *And Here's to You!* Among the many honors his books have received are: the International Reading Association Children's Choices Award; Bank Street College Best of the Best; Chicago Public Library Best of the Best; NY Public Library Best Books for Children; ALA Notable; and the Parents' Guide to Children's Media Award. David teaches at Lesley University, Cambridge, Massachusetts, where he is a faculty mentor in the low-residency MFA program in creative writing. This is David's second Gemma Open Door title; *The Tiger's Back* was published in 2012. Visit David at www.davidelliottbooks .com.

First published by GemmaMedia in 2014.

GemmaMedia
230 Commercial Street
Boston MA 02109 USA

www.gemmamedia.com

Printed in the United States of America

18 17 16 15 14 1 2 3 4 5

978-1-936846-49-8

Library of Congress Cataloging-in-Publication Data

Elliott, David, 1947–
Forever and Ever / David Elliott.
pages cm. — (Gemma Open Door)
ISBN 978-1-936846-49-8
1. Grief—Fiction. 2. Psychological fiction. I. Title.
PS3605.L4456F67 2014
813′.6—dc23

2014031710

Cover by Laura Shaw Design

Inspired by the Irish series designed for new readers, Gemma's Open Doors provide fresh stories, new ideas, and essential resources for young people and adults as they embrace the power of reading and the written word.

Brian Bouldrey
North American Series Editor

Open Door

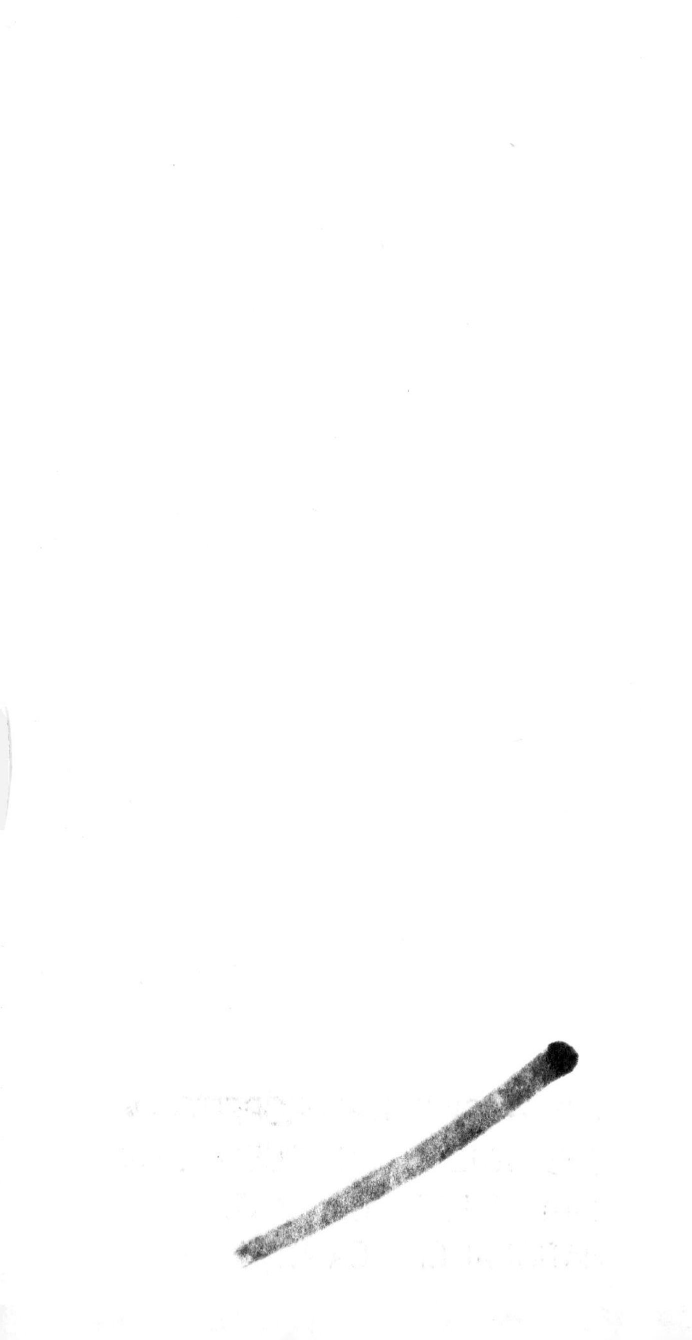

To all that haunts us.

ONE

Jaimie disliked John and Muriel Malabrand almost as much as he disliked his own parents, if such a thing were possible. But that wasn't why he balked when his mother said that John and Muriel wanted to talk to him. It was the mention of a surprise that had caused his stomach to turn. Jaimie was just sixteen, but he figured he'd had enough *surprise* to last the rest of his life.

The Malabrands could go screw themselves.

He tried to fake a headache, one of the migraines that after seventeen years of almost perfect health would flare up like a campfire left smoldering in the woods. The kind that left nothing behind but the charred ruins of a forest.

He walked into the kitchen with his hand to his temple, doing what he could to reproduce the scrim that blurred his vision whenever one of these attacks hit him. In her desperation to return to the way things were, his mother didn't notice.

She had scrambled what looked like a dozen eggs. *Why?* Jaimie asked himself. *Why does she do it?* He had no appetite. She knew that. Knew he wouldn't touch it. And yet every morning it was the same, enough protein on his plate to feed a village in India.

He slumped at the table, staring out the back window. A robin—the first he had seen this spring—was tugging at a night crawler. How long, he wondered?

How long would it take until the worm gave up its hold in the dark, wet earth? Or snapped in two?

Behind him, his mother rinsed the breakfast dishes.

"It might be nice for you to see what John and Muriel have in mind," she said. "They have always liked you. Everybody has always liked you." When he didn't respond, she added, "And anyway, it's not like you to be rude, Jaimie. You can't just ignore them."

Oh, but that's where she was wrong. He *could* ignore them. Shut them out the way he shut out everybody. His teachers. His friends. His mother. It was easy. All he had to do was close his eyes. Close his eyes and think of Jannie.

"Try to eat something, Jaimie," his

mother said. "You'll feel better. I know you will."

He shoved the plate aside. His mother had not approved of Jannie. Didn't think she was the right kind of girl. She had never said so, of course. She never would. But Jaimie could sense it, just as he could sense her disapproval of the clothes Jannie picked out for him and the streak of blue she had dyed into his hair.

He could refuse. Put his foot down. Tell his mother the Malabrands could take their surprise and shove it. Stop once and for all everybody trying to help him. He didn't need help. He needed Jannie. He only needed Jannie. But that kind of resistance took energy. Energy he didn't have. Not now. Maybe not ever again.

That was why, two days later, on a wet Saturday afternoon, he found himself slumped at the door of the Malabrands' grotesque McMansion. He raised a finger to the doorbell. John Malabrand loved that doorbell. Jaimie remembered his going on about it when they were building the house.

"You can program it," he had bragged to Jaimie's father. "You can actually program the damn thing! Thirty different tunes!"

Jaimie pressed the fake mother-of-pearl button. What would it be this time? "Home on the Range"? "La Cucaracha"? Or John's favorite, "Camptown Races"? But no. Of course. It was "London Bridge." John and Muriel had just come back from two weeks in England.

He was turning to leave when the door swung open.

"Jaimie boy!" John shouted. "You made it!"

Even from the doorstep, Jaimie could smell the booze.

But ten minutes later John and Muriel were offering him the use of their cottage on Lake Winnepocket, and he was glad he had come.

"It's nothin' fancy," John said.

They were sitting in the oddly-angled space that Muriel insisted on calling the great room. Its ceiling was cathedraled so high above them that, in spite of the windows, Jaimie felt as if he were trapped underground.

John was perched on a gigantic sectional sofa. Jaimie supposed the horrible green fringe that trimmed the couch was meant to complement the sickly color of the walls. Instead, it served to highlight the rash of exploded blood vessels that stretched over John's nose and oozed down his cheeks. The red blotch reminded Jaimie of maps of pandemics that were all over the Internet.

"Nope. Nothin' fancy," John repeated. "Just two rooms and a loo."

Loo?

Seriously?

The man had spent two weeks in England and suddenly he was talking like one of the Beatles.

"We bought the place furnished a couple of years ago," John went on. "Built in 1922. Thought we'd fix it up, but one thing led to another. I don't think we've gone up there but twice. Probably should sell it. Muriel never liked the place."

"It's in *New Hampshire*, for Chrissake," moaned Muriel, lighting another cigarette. "The mosquitoes! My god! The mosquitoes!"

Between her chain-smoking and her perfume, Jaimie didn't believe a mosquito could get within ten feet of her.

"And those ducks!" Muriel said.

She took a long pull on her cigarette.

"Loons," her husband corrected.

"Honestly, it's like the criminally insane are out there paddling around in the dark. No thanks." She turned to Jaimie. "I understand why you might want to spend a week or two up there in Godforsaken, New Hampshire. After everything you've gone through, I mean.

But between you and me, Jaimie, I've squashed my last mosquito and heard the gibbering of my last duck."

"Loon," John said again.

Muriel stood up and walked into the kitchen. A stainless steel nightmare. Like the inside of a UFO, Jaimie thought. For a second he imagined a spaceship filled with Muriel clones. Terrifying.

She mixed herself another drink as John gave Jaimie instructions for the cottage, detailing its many quirks.

"I'll tell Moses Eldred to put a key under the mat," John said. "He's the local who looks after the place for us. And don't try to open the back door. You'll never get it shut."

Jaimie stood up to go.

"Oh, I almost forgot," John added.

He steadied himself on an end table. "The water in all the faucets will run brown the first day or so."

"Like blood," Muriel yelled from the kitchen.

TWO

After everything you've gone through.

The words stayed with Jaimie. They were with him now as he headed out of Boston, driving north to New Hampshire. He could hear Muriel's smoke-ravaged voice. Could see her downturned lips.

Muriel was clueless. Like everybody else. His parents. Barry Pryce. His friends. Why couldn't they see it? He hadn't gone through anything. That was the point. There *was* no going through. Jannie was dead. There was no going anywhere.

His lips twisted into a half smile. He was thinking of the way he'd tricked Barry Pryce. Barry Pryce. PhD. The so-called grief counselor his parents made him see after the accident.

The man was a dick. Him and his five stages of grief. As if what Jaimie was feeling was nothing more than a recipe in one of the glossy magazines his mother fanned so precisely on the coffee table.

Want a surefire fix when the love of your life kicks the bucket? Follow these five easy steps and you'll be twerking on her grave in no time.

Start with a healthy dollop of denial.

Now shake in a little anger.

"I'm feeling better," Jaimie had lied in his last session with Pryce. He was good at lying now. And why not? With Jannie gone, it was all a lie. Getting up in the morning. Brushing his teeth. Please.

Thank you. Yes. No. All of it. "My appetite is coming back, too."

Pryce smiled and bobbed his head. He reminded Jaimie of a weird toy ostrich. The legless kind that dunks its head in water.

"Right on schedule," he had said to Jaimie. "You've moved through the first four stages. Now, you're entering the final one: Acceptance. Right on schedule."

Jaimie tried to assume the posture of someone dumb enough to swallow this BS.

"Thank you for your help," he said. "It's . . . it's been rough."

Pryce continued to nod and smile. Jaimie had him right where he wanted him. His parents would never let him spend a week at the cottage alone unless Pryce approved it.

He'd thrown out the bait. Now it was time to hook the bastard.

"I . . . I really feel like I could use some time to myself. You know . . . to get my head back together and everything."

"That's only natural," the doctor said. "You deserve it."

And that was that.

Jaimie pulled into the left lane to pass a white, late-model Ford puttering along at forty-five miles an hour. He accelerated as he turned his head to check out the driver. His breath stopped so suddenly that, for a moment, he thought he might pass out.

An old woman sat hunched in the driver's seat. Her upper body leaning toward the windshield. Her fingers curling around the steering wheel. Her fingers, with their gross, swollen knuckles. Like leeches, he thought.

He lowered his speed so that his Volvo ran parallel to the Ford.

One mile.

Two.

With each click of the odometer, his rage burned hotter. She had to be in her eighties. Older even than the old man who had run the stop sign. The man who had killed Jannie.

What was that old bag doing behind the wheel of a car? She had no right. Any fool could see that. She was too old. Too old to live even. Why was she alive and Jannie gone? Hadn't he and Jannie sworn they would never be apart? Hadn't his classmates voted them The Couple Most Likely to Stay Together? Jannie and Jaimie. Jaimie and Jannie. That's the way it was supposed to be. Forever. Forever and ever.

What would it feel like to run the old woman off the road just the way the old man had run Jannie off the road? See her go through the windshield just the way the police said that Jannie had? Watch her choke on her own blood?

It would be easy. The slightest downward pull of his right arm. That's all it would take. Easy! Easy-peasy! Easier, when he thought about it, than not doing it. He tightened his grip. The Volvo inched closer to the center line.

If she so much as glances at me I'll do it, he thought. *Swear to God! I will!*

He brought the Volvo so close to the old woman's car that if the windows had been open, he could have flicked her on the temple.

Look at me! Look at me!

But the old woman kept her eyes straight ahead. She didn't even know he was there.

He stomped on the accelerator.

The Ford disappeared behind him.

THREE

Welcome to New Hampshire, the sign said. *Bienvenue!*

Bienvenue . . . Bienvenue . . .

Jaimie's mind went to junior year French, the only class he and Jannie had ever taken together. Jaimie was an honors student. Almost certainly bound for a school like Middlebury or Reed. Jannie stuck to vocational courses. If he hadn't forced her, she never would have enrolled in a language class.

"I'm not the type," she had said.

"But it will be fun. We'll sit together. I'll help you with your homework. Besides, look at your last name. Gagnon."

He pronounced it the way a native French speaker would have. Emphasizing the nasal at the end. Jannie pronounced it the way all New Englanders did. Gag-nun.

"Gagnon," he said again. "With a name like that, you're halfway there."

Madame Stanley had taken an instant dislike to Jannie. It didn't help that Jannie fell asleep during the drills. And even Jaimie could hear the train wreck that was her accent. The harsh "*r*'s." The plosive consonants. Was it that she had no ear for it? Or did she simply make no effort?

Still, they loved to practice dialogues that Jaimie pulled from the grammar and vocabulary Madame Stanley drummed into them. In those manufactured conversations, Jannie would pretend to be an exchange student visiting Paris.

Or a teacher from St. Louis. Once she was a nurse. Jaimie, however, would always play the same part. The young Frenchman overcome by the beauty and charm of an American girl.

While the details of these simple exercises changed, the pattern never varied. It began with Jaimie introducing himself to Jannie, who would be lost on the Left Bank. Or confused about which subway to take to get to the Eiffel Tower. Or looking for a particular restaurant near Notre Dame. But no matter how the dialogue started, it ended with the same five words: "*Je t'aime, Jannie, je t'aime.*"

"Tell me again, Jaimie," Jannie would whisper. "Say it again."

Jaimie got an A in French; Jannie barely passed.

Jaimie scanned the landscape on either side of the highway. Hemlocks. Pines. The occasional birch or maple. So many trees. Like soldiers. One battalion after another marching down to the very edge of the highway.

He was struck with the odd sense that he had been on this stretch of road before. Maybe on his way to a summer camp. Or a school field trip. His mother insisted that he had never crossed the state line. "Unless, of course, you and Jannie drove up there," she'd said. *Drove.* That's what she said. But Jaimie knew what she meant: *snuck.* He'd heard it in her voice. He was sure of it. *Snuck up there*.

When he'd left the house, earlier that afternoon, the sun shone so brightly that even the shadows seemed reflective. But across the border, a dirty gray blanketed the sky. The farther north he drove, the heavier the mist that settled over the landscape.

He switched on the wipers.

Once he was off the highway, he kept a lookout out for landmarks. Yes, there was the farm stand next to the ramshackle colonial house with the peeling white paint. *The Courser Farm*, the sign read. According to John Malabrand's directions, he was only a couple of miles from the cottage.

The car veered to the left as he jammed his foot on the brake. His right hand shot out to protect the laptop, loose in the passenger seat beside him.

As if summoned out of the mist, a

trio of deer burst onto the road. Two does and a huge buck. He missed colliding with the buck by a matter of inches. So close that Jaimie saw his own reflection in the terror of the animal's eye. He slowed down.

FOUR

The cottage sat by itself on an isolated spit of sandy grass at the dead end of an unmarked dirt road. John had been right. It wasn't fancy. A squat, shingled box with a porch attached as an afterthought to the front. A thick stand of evergreens encroached on the back wall, their lower branches reaching out as if to tag the cabin's rusting tin roof. Pinecones littered the ground in front of the porch. A party quickly abandoned.

The long, narrow lake stretched out in front of him.

Jannie would have loved it here, he thought.

He remembered the first time he saw her in the water. Her long, thin torso, buoyant and lithe. Her legs softly churning behind her. And all the while, the steady rhythm of her arms, slender and white, entering and leaving the surface as effortlessly as blades of a windmill slicing through fog. She was more herself in a lake, she had told him, than on dry land.

Jaimie had tried to convince her to join the school swim team. *You could get a scholarship to a great college*, he had said more than once. *You're that good.* She wasn't interested. *I'm not going to college.* That was all she'd said.

Jaimie was not a swimmer. When he was a boy, he had nearly drowned when his older cousin dunked him one too many times. He still didn't like to put his head underwater.

A finger of lightning snaked across the sky. A deafening clap of thunder. The mist had finally resolved itself into a proper storm. Rain. Hard and loud. Sounding more like hail than raindrops pelting the roof of the Volvo. Another bolt of lightning.

Involuntarily, his left hand grabbed the steering wheel.

It was impossible.

He had seen someone.

In the lake.

A lone swimmer.

An arm in mid-stroke extended above the head.

Even a city boy like Jaimie knew how dangerous it was to be in the water during a storm. He moved closer to the windshield, squinting through the rain.

The explosive crack of a lightning strike somewhere behind him caused him to jerk back.

He scanned the surface of the water.

No one.

Some cosmic magician had pulled off a magnificent stunt. *Now you see it. Now you don't.*

He looked again toward the spot where he had seen the swimmer. But the rain was falling so hard it was impossible to focus more than a few feet out from the shore.

He must have imagined the whole thing. Just the way he'd imagined he'd been on the road that brought him here. Maybe he'd seen one of those loons Muriel had talked about, mistaking it for a human. That had to be it.

Still, the swimmer or loon or whatever it was had spooked him, as if he were the butt of some terrible joke. He thought about the deer he had nearly hit just a few moments ago. The way the animal had looked at him. The panic in its eye. And for the first time since he had heard about the cottage, he wondered if it were such a good idea to have come.

FIVE

It was as if the cottage had been holding its breath. A rush of stale, mildewed air hit him.

"Jesus," he said from the rotting porch.

He squinted into the half light of the room's interior.

It looked like a set from an amateur theater production. A faded sofa sagged deeply in the middle, like it was grinning at him. A matching chair. Cheap paneling. A stray rocker.

He stepped into the room.

The floor tilted crazily away from the shoreline.

To his right, a wooden table sat under a small window facing the lake. Someone had stuck a book of matches under one of its scarred legs. He brushed away the dead flies littering the table's surface and set his laptop down in the space he had cleared.

Shades covered the other windows, two of which faced the lake. Fly-specked. Streaked with dust. The shades fluttered limply. He went to the nearest, hoping to get a little light into the dismal interior. But he pulled too hard. The roller came out of its brackets. It bounced on the linoleum floor and onto his sandaled foot.

"Shit!"

The metal pin at the end of the dowel had gouged a chunk out of his foot. It stung like hell. More shocking than the jab of pain had been the noise that disturbed the silence locked in the cottage since John and Muriel's last visit. The crack of the wooden dowel hitting the floor and then the sharp sound of his own voice. He looked over his shoulder.

Screw the windows.

He pulled a yellow sweater from his duffle bag.

Jannie had made the sweater for him. A birthday present. Her first and last effort. It was two sizes too big and the wool was so heavy and rough that the back of his neck broke out in a rash the first time he wore it. His mother said that the color made him look sallow. Sallow. He wasn't even sure what it meant.

He slipped the sweater over his tee and tossed his sleeping bag on the couch. There was a bedroom at the back of the cottage. But he would sleep anywhere rather than in a bed in which John and Muriel might have had sex. He switched on a tarnished candlestick lamp that sat in the middle of the wooden table. He opened his laptop, turned on the power, and sat down on a spindled chair. Someone—Muriel?—had painted it a fluorescent pink. The lurid color didn't stand a chance against the bullying gloom of the cottage. The chair was obscene in its manufactured cheer, pornographic.

"There's electricity, of course," John Malabrand had told him. "But you won't get reception for your cell. And if you want the Internet, you'll have to go to the library in the village. No connection at the cottage."

Waiting for his desktop to appear, he stared out at the lake, looking directly at the spot where he thought he had seen the swimmer. Nothing. Just the choppy surface, and the heavy, granite-colored sky above it.

What kind of fish were in the lake? Bass, maybe. Bluegills. Perch. He imagined them swimming through the dark water. Not conscious they were alive until a snapping turtle got them. Or hooks yanked them out of the water.

Did Jannie know? he asked himself, not for the first time. Did she know she was being yanked out of the lake when the old man hit her?

He turned back to the laptop and opened a folder. Calculus Homework.

He moved his cursor to the single file and clicked twice.

A picture of Jannie appeared on the screen. Her tenth birthday. On the picnic table in front of her, a single piece of cake listed dangerously to the left, as if it wanted to lie down and sleep. Jannie looked directly into the camera. Smiling. Even at a party, her eyes held that same quality that had attracted Jaimie the first day they met. Melancholy? Anger? Or some other emotion Jaimie had no name for.

Jannie's father had left her with her hard-drinking mother when Jannie was five.

"The day he left, he gave me a teddy bear," she told him. "It was purple. Like an Easter egg." When Jaimie asked what happened to it, she said she'd thrown it away. "My favorite color was red. He should have known that."

The snapshot lingered for a moment and then faded as the next took its place. Jannie in a cap and gown. Graduating from middle school. Her thick black hair stuck out from the miniature mortarboard like a fright wig. "I told you," she'd said to Jaimie when she'd given these pictures to him. "I'm part Gypsy."

A more recent picture appeared on the screen, Jannie leaning into him at a school dance. The sleeves of his rented tuxedo were an inch too short. The tie and cummerbund matched the electric crimson of Jannie's dress. He would never forget that night. "Tell me again, Jaimie. Say it again." His fingertips brushed the screen. *Jannie,* he whispered. *Jannie.*

Next came a series of selfies that Jannie called her "special" pictures. These almost always landed in his inbox late on a weeknight. Jaimie hadn't known how to respond when the first of these arrived with the subject heading *For You're Eyes Only*. But later, once he was more used to them, he looked forward to their dark, forbidden thrill. So what if she'd made an error with the pronoun? *You're* instead of *Your*. She'd taken them for *him*. For His Eyes Only. That's what mattered. Not some stupid mistake.

He had thought about deleting these pictures. What if his mother found them? But now he was glad he hadn't.

It would serve his mother right if she did find them. *Snuck up there*. That's what she'd meant.

He pulled his chair closer to the table. Another set of pictures was starting. His favorites. Taken last year in Vermont when Jannie had convinced him to cut classes for the day. At first, he'd said it was impossible. He had a midterm in Bewley's fourth-period American history. But Jannie had looked so disappointed that he bypassed the entrance to the school parking lot and headed toward the interstate leading north. He only thought of the test again when well into Vermont, as they passed a monument to the soldiers of the Revolutionary War.

The cycle of pictures ended and began

again. And then again. This was why he had come. To be alone. Alone with Jannie. Without the phone calls asking if he'd like to go to some stupid movie. Or his father's pressing him to watch the game with him. Or his mother's constant nagging to eat more. (The box of groceries his mother had packed for him was still on the Volvo's back seat. "Don't forget to eat," she'd begged. "Promise me you'll eat while you're up there.")

He felt giddy, almost like a kid again.

Jannie and Jaimie.

Jaimie and Jannie.

Forever.

Forever and ever.

SIX

By the time he stood up from his computer, Jaimie's legs were stiff. He stepped onto the porch. The rain had finally stopped. Overhead, thick clouds covered the moon. A silver mist hovered over the lake.

He shivered. The Malabrands had warned him that the nights could get chilly on Winnepocket, but he hadn't been expecting this. For a moment, he thought he could see his breath. But it was only orphaned pockets of mist drifting away from the lake onto the beach.

The water was calm. He looked to the spot where he thought he had seen the swimmer. Nothing.

Still shivering, he went back inside,

switched out the light, and crawled into the sleeping bag fully dressed. He and Jannie had spent more than one night in this sleeping bag. If he concentrated, he could sometimes smell the faint trace of her perfume. Why wasn't she here with him now? Her hair tucked behind her ear. Her eyes half-closed in the first moments of their lovemaking.

A series of disembodied pitches floated through the dark, wet air. He sat up. A horse, maybe two, across the lake. In some kind of trouble. Screaming. His heart was racing. Then he remembered. No, not horses. Loons.

Hoo-hoo-hoo-ho-hoo-hoooooo.

Hoo-hoo-hoo-ho-hoo-hooooo.

Before Jaimie left Framingham, he had Googled images of the birds. With their speckled backs and long, graceful necks, they were beautiful. There was no denying that. But there was something primitive about them, too. The blackness of their heads, the long, narrow beaks tapering to sharp points. And in many of the photos, mostly taken by amateurs, their eyes looked red. He pictured them out there now, floating on the surface of the black water, invisible in the mist.

Over and over they called.

Hoo-hoo-hoo-ho-hoo-hoooooo.

Hoo-hoo-hoo-ho-hoo-hooooo.

Eventually, Jaimie lay back down.

Ignoring the sweat that had dampened his back and arms, he pulled the sleeping bag up around his ears and drifted into a fitful sleep.

SEVEN

Was it the chill that awakened him?

Or the calling of the loons?

Once.

Twice.

Jaimie finally lost count.

Hoo-hoo-hoo-ho-hoo-hoo.

Hoo-hoo-hoo-ho-hoo-hoo.

Two birds, he thought. One crying out. The other answering. The silence between the calls as unnerving as the eerie sound of the birds themselves.

What had Muriel said? *Like the criminally insane out there paddling around in the dark.* But Muriel was wrong. The back and forth of the birds was the opposite of insanity. As natural as their flying south in the winter—if that's what they did—or raising their young. He knew that as surely as he knew his own name. Or Jannie's.

Why then did he want it to stop?

He lay in the darkness of the unfamiliar room trying not to listen. Hoping that each call would be the last. But the cries continued. Echoing across the lake. Bouncing off the cabin's dark walls. Over and over.

Hoo-hoo-hoo-ho-hoo-hoo.

Hoo-hoo-hoo-ho-hoo-hoo.

It was as if the loons were caught in a loop, stuck in a pattern from which they could never escape. Like Kyle Jensen, the autistic boy who, for a short time, had been mainstreamed into Jaimie's fifth-grade classroom. Jaimie had tried to befriend the boy, but no matter what he said, what he tried, Kyle's response was always the same: three lines from an animated movie.

Jaimie shifted his right leg. The noise of his jeans sliding across the nylon lining made him stop. The loons were reminding him of something else. Something he wanted to forget. The time he had gone to Mass with Jannie.

Jaimie's family was not religious. Except for the occasional wedding of a relative, Jaimie had never been in a church. And never at a Catholic Mass. So when Jannie had asked him to go with her, he was excited. Should be fun, he thought.

The moment he entered Our Lady of the Angels, he was creeped out. The heavy scent of incense crowded what little oxygen there was in the place. And people, people he knew, Mr. Bewley, for instance, kept staring at him. Smiling, as if they shared a secret. He didn't like it. It reminded him of an old sci-fi movie that had scared the pants off him.

He could still see the priest in his purple vestments, his arms raised above the faithful. And behind him, the life-sized crucifix. The shining, pale skin of the crucified one. The half-opened eyes. The blood. The nails. And Jannie, *his* Jannie, no longer really with him, but a part of the anonymous congregation. Like some kind of insect fulfilling the destiny of its colony. Kneeling. Bowing her head. Repeating the priest's supplications for mercy.

Lord have mercy.

Christ have mercy.

It had frightened him, this calling down of the other world. Made him feel so alone that he could almost see the invisible wall separating him from the others. From Jannie. No, not one wall. But four. A closet. A casket. He hadn't been able to sleep that night. Or the next. Or many nights that followed.

Jannie had teased him about it. Called him crazy. A sissy. Told him God would punish him. Send him to hell. But even so, he wouldn't go back. It was the only thing he had ever refused her.

Oddly, she didn't seem to mind.

"Don't worry about it," she'd say. "You'll come around one day. I'll get you sooner or later."

Now, the loons' mimicking the call

and response of the believers both
mocked and justified the fear he felt
that morning at Our Lady of the Angels.

He tried to swallow but couldn't.
Hoo-hoo-hoo-ho-hoo-hoo.
Hoo-hoo-hoo-ho-hoo-hoo.
Lord have mercy.
Christ have mercy.

EIGHT

Someone was knocking on the door. He opened his eyes, squinting. Yesterday's unsettled weather had been replaced with bright sunshine. He looked at his watch.

11:33.

He squirmed out of his sleeping bag, still dressed in the yellow sweater and jeans, and stumbled in his stocking feet toward the door. Through the old bubbled glass and the filmy grain of the screen in front of it, Jaimie saw a man, balding, his hair grown long at the back and sides and unashamedly noodled over the front. A beard but no moustache.

Jaimie opened the door, leaving the screen between himself and the stranger.

"Name's Eldred," the man said. "Moses Eldred."

He smiled.

Jaimie blinked. Moses Eldred was missing a tooth. The third one back on the left side. The remaining teeth were blazingly white.

"I keep an eye out on the place for John Malabrand," he said in a Yankee accent so thick that for a moment Jaimie wondered if was speaking English. "I live ovah theyah." The man turned and pointed a thick finger to a peninsula jutting out from the shore about a quarter mile from where the cottage stood. "Right through them trees. Deepest part of the lake."

As if Jaimie's silence were an invitation, Moses Eldred pulled back the screen and stepped into the cottage. He pointed his chin toward Jaimie's laptop.

"How much RAM you got on that thing?" he asked.

It wasn't a question Jaimie had been expecting.

"Four," he finally said.

Moses Eldred raised his eyebrows and smiled. Once again, the impossible whiteness of the man's teeth.

"Got eight on mine," Eldred said.

Jaimie didn't know how to reply. One thing was certain. He wasn't about to get in a pissing contest with Moses Eldred over who had the most manly computer.

"The loons were kind of noisy last night," he finally mumbled. It was an idiotic thing to say. "I had a hard time sleeping."

Moses Eldred paused as if he were about to say something, then seemed to reconsider. He took a turn around the room, looking questioningly at Jaimie when he saw the roller from the blind that still lay where it had fallen. Then, apparently satisfied that nothing more was amiss, he walked out of the cottage as abruptly as he had walked in. But not without taking one last peek at Jaimie's laptop. Standing on the lawn, damp from yesterday's storm, he looked up at Jaimie behind the screen.

"I didn't heayah a thin' last night," he said.

"The loons? You didn't hear them?"

"Audubon fellah just out heayah," Moses Eldred said. "No loons on the lake this yeayah."

Jaimie stared at the man.

"But I heard them," he said.

"Don't know what you heard, sonny, but it weren't no loons. I'll guarantee you that. Audubon fellah couldn't find a one of 'em. No nests neitha." He looked over at Jaimie's Volvo. "I'd move that from under them pines if I was you," he said. "Sap'll drip right on it. Ruin the paint."

With that, Moses Eldred ambled to his truck, a beat-up Chevy with the license plate hanging at a forty-five-degree angle. Jaimie read the state motto printed at the bottom of the plate: Live Free or Die.

NINE

"I live ovah they-ah," Jaimie said in an exaggerated imitation of Moses Eldred's Yankee dialect. If only Jannie had been here to have heard him. "Right ovah they-ah," Jaimie said again. "Local yokel."

He spent the rest of the afternoon listening to playlists he and Jannie had made together, looking at the pictures again, reading through the hundreds of cards and notes she'd sent him. He traced her childish signature with the tip of his finger.

Je t'aime, Jannie, je t'aime.

Occasionally, the business with the loons would come back to him, and he felt a quick charge of the fear he'd felt last night. But he'd come here to be with Jannie. Not to freak out over some stupid nature thing. Moses Eldred didn't know what he was talking about. It was probably mating season or something. When he got back to civilization he'd do a little research.

As for Moses Eldred himself, he could take his idiotic hair, his weird white teeth, and his eight RAMs of memory and shove them. The man couldn't even speak English. Probably hadn't finished high school. *If I really love Jannie*, he told himself, *I'll forget about Moses Eldred and the whole stupid thing with the loons. Anyway, I was probably dreaming.*

At sunset, he stepped out of the cottage. The sky was cloudless, fading from its all-day blue to rose, almost as if it had embarrassed itself with so much good cheer. The surface of the lake was smooth and reflected the sky so brilliantly it looked burnished. No mysterious swimmers. No loons that didn't exist. Jaimie stood there for several minutes. The lowering sun warmed his face and arms.

He'd been right. This was what he needed all along. This time with Jannie. Alone. Without his mother's constant questions about his state of mind. Without his father's false good cheer and well-meaning invitations to a movie or ballgame. Without Barry Pryce and his BS. Without the pitying, fearful glances from the friends he and Jannie used to have. Without having to pretend that everything was normal.

Nothing was normal. It never would be. Jannie would be a part of him as long as he lived. He knew that. Standing there on the edge of the calm lake, something shifted inside him. Maybe his longing for Jannie wouldn't always be as painful as it was now. Maybe somehow he would get through it.

It wasn't an epiphany, this feeling. Nothing as strong as that. Just a slight stirring. Like a sleeper who knows he has a busy day ahead of him, and that sometime, sometime soon perhaps, he will have to wake up.

For the first time in months, Jaimie was hungry.

The milk his mother had packed was surely sour by now. But he knew there was a loaf of freshly baked banana bread in the carton on the back seat. Other things, too. And while he was at it, he might as well move the car away from the trees. Moses Eldred was a local yokel, but there was no sense in allowing the trees to ruin the finish on the Volvo.

He walked across the sandy lawn. As he reached to open the front door of the car, a pinecone fell. A big one. It hit his forearm with such force that one of its woody scales raked a scratch diagonally midway between his elbow and his wrist.

Jaimie yelped. The pinecone had startled him, and the scrape hurt like hell. Then he remembered. The pinecone had struck his arm at just the spot that Jannie had injured a month or so before the accident.

It wasn't her fault. Not really. He'd

been in the library, leaning over the back of Ashley Whittlinger's chair, his forearm resting on the table. He was pointing out where Ashley was going wrong with a math problem. Innocent, but Jannie had seen and misunderstood. Before he could explain, she'd picked up a heavy research volume and slammed it down on his forearm. Later, he and Jannie had laughed about it, joking about her Gypsy temper. He told his mother he'd gotten the bruise in PE class.

Another cone fell. This one landing at his feet. He looked up into the trees, expecting to see a squirrel. Suddenly, all the cones in the towering pine released. All of them. All at once. Like a storm cloud had opened directly above him. A cloud filled with heavy, stinging cones rained down on him. He jumped backward, but not before several of the cones had left their marks.

For a moment, he stood still. Stunned. An uneven ring of pinecones surrounded the Volvo. Some of them were as big as shoes. He was breathing hard.

Things like this happen all the time in nature, he told himself. *They're always saying that on those nature shows on TV. How nature is mysterious, unpredictable.*

If he looked hard enough, he knew he would find a logical explanation for it.

Forgetting about his hunger, he went back to the cottage, leaving the banana bread on the back seat of the Volvo.

TEN

That night, he lay on his back. Eyes shut. His teeth chattering in spite of the sleeping bag. The call of the loons echoed over the water.

Moses Eldred had been trying to frighten him. That was it. He'd heard about these old-time Yankees and their weird sense of humor. He'd also heard that they didn't much like summer people. Their city ways. Their easy money. Gawking at the locals. Moses Eldred was probably lying in his bed right now, laughing his ass off as he thought about the city boy over there in Malabrand's cottage listening to the loons that he'd said didn't exist.

He opened his eyes.

Somewhere in the cabin, a light was on.

His eyes must have been playing tricks on him. He was sure he'd turned the lamp off before he crawled into his sleeping bag. In fact, with the moon behind the clouds, he remembered thinking how dark it was in the cabin. As if the entire universe had gone blind.

He turned his head to the left.

The computer screen cast a blue glow onto the surface of the table. That was the source of the light. He must have forgotten to turn it off. The desktop was frozen on a blank screen. He wrenched himself out of the tangle of the sleeping bag and padded over to the table.

The screen wasn't blank. A photograph filled its black frame. Water. A lake maybe, or a pond. The photo was little more than a rectangle divided into two halves. The upper half a cloudless sky. The bottom half the surface of the calm water. The photographer had captured a ripple in the left foreground as if he (or she?) had suddenly dipped an arm below the surface.

Jaimie swallowed, trying to keep down the sour taste rising from his stomach. He had never seen this picture.

He sat in the pink chair and studied the photograph. There was nothing to distinguish it. No rough edge of shore. No boats. Not even a cloud in the sky. It could have been any body of water anywhere in the world. And now its image was on his laptop.

He looked up, wishing he had locked the door.

He put his hand on the mouse, trying not to notice that his fingers were trembling. When he clicked forward, the photo faded and was replaced by a familiar one. Jannie. That day in Vermont. Sitting at a picnic table at a state park. When he clicked back, the picture of the water was gone.

Out on Winnepocket, the loons called to each other. It sounded like they were laughing.

ELEVEN

Jaimie spent most of the next day in bed. He'd stayed up nearly until dawn searching his laptop for the mysterious picture of the lake. But it had disappeared. After several hours, he'd begun to wonder if he had seen it in the first place.

It was like the experience of repeating a familiar word over and over again. Something he had marveled at as a kid. If you said it long enough, the word lost its meaning. Take any word. Lightbulb. Say it again and again. It might mean anything.

Or nothing.

Looking for the phantom image was like repeating a word into nothingness. By the time he gave up, his search for the picture had no meaning. He wasn't even sure why he'd begun it in the first place.

He'd finally dragged himself back to his sleeping bag an hour or two before dawn. Exhausted, freezing, and with the arc of flashing light that signaled the beginning of a migraine. When he woke up, several hours later, his head was pounding.

Until the accident, Jaimie had never been prone to headaches. Or any illness really. Not even an allergy. His mother still had his certificate for perfect attendance from his elementary school.

The first one hit the day after Jannie's funeral. After the third attack, the night before his first visit with Barry Pryce, his mother made an appointment with a specialist in Boston. But she couldn't get Jaimie in until the week following his trip to Winnepocket.

The pain raged at the top of his skull. Drilled against his temples. Waves of nausea swept through him. One minute his limbs were lashed to slabs of granite. The next, they had been amputated.

A new sensation began to wash over him. The pain was there, yes, but *he* wasn't. The headache had relieved him from his body and transported him to some other dimension while it stayed behind to do the heavy lifting. And in this new dimension, he was with Jannie. Just like old times.

They talked and laughed just like before. They walked along the lake, then floated out into its center, their spirits as buoyant as their bodies. They even practiced one of their French dialogues. *Say it again, Jaimie. Tell me again.* There seemed to be no time in this place where the migraine had taken him. No beginnings. No endings. Each moment seemed complete and, at the same time, a part of some larger expression of itself. *Jannie and Jaimie. Jaimie and Jannie. Forever. Forever and ever.*

At some point—how long had he been in this elevated state?—he began to feel a pull back and was filled with a sadness so deep and so heavy, he wondered if he were the one who had died. He could feel Jannie trying to hold on. But it was no use. She was gone.

The headache finally subsided just as the sun was setting over the lake. Jaimie felt like he always did after these episodes. As if he'd been emptied of himself. As if he had to start all over again. Learning who he was. His name. His age. His memories. Who and what he loved. Filling in all the blanks.

He had perspired so heavily during the migraine that his hair was stuck to his forehead. His skin was ticklish. He pulled his legs out of the nylon cocoon, swung them over the side of the couch, and stood up. He was light-headed and half expected to levitate. The headaches always left him feeling like this. Weightless. And thirsty.

He went to the sink, got himself a glass of water, and drank it down in one long draft. Then he splashed some of the cool water on his face and drank some more. This time he didn't bother with a glass. He slurped the water from the tap the way his mother would never permit at home.

He looked at the laptop, still on the table in Sleep mode.

Had he seen the photograph or not? Was the whole episode just some weird precursor to the migraine? The headache was the worst he'd had. By far. People report seeing all kinds of strange things before severe headaches hit. Maybe the incident with the picture was normal. Or at least on the outer edges of normal. He'd ask the specialist about it.

Then he remembered something he had heard in Mrs. Matson's sophomore psychology class. How native people would fast in order to bring on the hallucinations that would guide them during vision quests. Maybe that's what was happening. He was hallucinating because he wasn't eating.

Once again, he felt hungry. Ravenous.

He opened a cupboard and found a carton of cheese and peanut butter crackers. The kind mothers buy to pack in their kids' lunches. The thought of Muriel buying such things struck him as comical. Partly because the color of her skin, the result of so much time spent in tanning booths, was just a shade or two away from the unnatural orange of the crackers. He grabbed the carton, ripped open its thin cardboard top, and pried out one of the packages from the bundle.

Delicious. Not as good as the banana bread, still in the Volvo. But luscious nonetheless.

Without bothering to wipe away the orange crumbs that had settled into the corners of his mouth, he pulled back the red cellophane strip from another pack and wolfed it down. And a third.

He definitely felt better. More like himself even since before Jannie died.

There had never been a phantom picture. He was sure of that now. He'd drummed it up on his own because of the lack of food. And that was probably what that business with the loons was about, too. Moses Eldred hadn't been tricking him. He'd imagined it. He'd imagined all of it.

He knew, too, that he hadn't actually been with Jannie when the migraine was on him. That he hadn't actually put his arm around her waist or kissed her forehead. That they hadn't walked along the lake together, his hand coupled over hers. Or floated out on the warm surface of the water to the point that Moses Eldred had said was the deepest part of the lake. He knew none of that had happened. That it had been some weird complication of the headache.

But the experience had changed him.

Once again, he understood that his love for Jannie would never go away. But that somehow it would find a place in his life. He was going to be all right. His senior year was coming up. It wouldn't be the same without her, but he would get through it. He would take Mrs. Matson's AP psychology class. Maybe he would even declare psych as his major when he went away to college.

And maybe his parents and his friends weren't so bad after all. They'd only been trying to help. Maybe Barry Pryce had been right all along. It was Jaimie who had been off-center, distorted by his own grief. (Pryce was still a dick, though. That would never change.)

Jaimie loved Jannie. He would always love her. She was gone, and there was nothing he could do to bring her back. He would live with her memory the rest of his life. But he would go on.

He turned off the laptop, closed its screen over the keyboard until he heard the soft click of the latch. Then, he went back to bed. He would get a good night's sleep, and first thing tomorrow, he would pack up and go home.

TWELVE

This time there was no doubt. The loons woke him. Louder now. Much louder. Were they behind him? Was there a channel of water that snaked around the back of the cottage? A narrow channel he had somehow missed? They were drawing nearer. Jaimie lay in his sleeping bag, certain that the primitive birds could see him, that they were in the cabin, that they were watching him.

He opened his eyes.

The noise stopped. All at once. As if a conductor had suddenly lowered his baton at the very peak of a symphony's most dramatic moment. Jaimie waited, afraid it would start up again. But he found no comfort in the silence that followed.

Nothing. Not the croak of a frog, the scrape of a cricket. He lay awake, listening, waiting, watching the moonlight as it broke through the clouds and cast its cold glow into the cottage and on all its lonely furnishings.

The laptop was on.

This time the screen showed a picture he recognized. The one of Jannie and him at the prom. Its familiarity silenced for a moment the panic that was clanging in his chest. Even as he watched, the prom picture faded. It was replaced by the photo of the lake.

The linoleum was cold on his bare feet as he walked to the laptop. The picture was exactly as it had been the night before. Almost abstract. Like a painting by that artist he'd learned about in art history.

He studied the image, forcing his eyes to go to every inch of its pixilated surface. Finally, he saw what he had not seen before. Just beneath the ripple in the foreground, the faint shadow of a hand. The barest outline of fingertips.

His stomach surged. He ran onto the porch and vomited.

He would know those fingers anywhere. How many times had he kissed them? Held them? How many times had they lain against his skin?

"Jannie," he whispered, leaning over the wooden railing, "Jannie."

The temperature seemed to be dropping a degree a minute. He went back inside, back to the laptop. Now the entire hand was visible just inches beneath the surface, palm up, the delicate fingers extended and slightly curled, beckoning.

He turned to the window.

The moonlight shone brightly on the lake and Jaimie could see far out over its surface. He blinked and looked back to the computer screen. How could he have been so stupid? The photograph. It wasn't of *any* lake, but *this* one. Lake Winnepocket. It had been taken from just where he was looking now, out by the peninsula where Moses Eldred said he lived.

For a moment he did nothing, thought nothing, felt nothing. Then he stood up. He walked out onto the porch and down the steps. He didn't stop until he stood at the shore of the lake.

He had been expecting it, waiting for it even. Her arm. Rising slowly out of the water, white as marble in the moonlight. He thought he would be sick again. But then the silvery light caught her legs, her beautiful legs, barely breaking the surface of the calm lake, and his fear left him.

He understood now. She had come here for him just the way he had come here for her. The local yokel was right. It wasn't the loons. It was Jannie. Jannie, calling for him.

His first step into the lake was so cold it took his breath away. But that wasn't important. Nothing was important. Only Jannie swimming back and forth in the moonlight, waiting for him. He remembered the look on his cousin's face that day so long ago when he pushed Jaimie's head underwater for what felt like the hundredth time. He wished his cousin could be here now. To see him, to see him moving through the deep, cold lake to be with Jannie.

The sandy bottom turned to muck. It slid up and over his ankles. Mid-chest now, the water wicked up into the heavy wool of the sweater, pulling him down.

He could hear her calling his name, *their* names.

Jannie and Jaimie.

Jaimie and Jannie.

Forever.

Forever and ever.

CPSIA information can be obtained
at www.ICGtesting.com
Printed in the USA
BVHW080358070322
630727BV00002B/84